For Rosemary

First U.S. edition 1994

Atheneum
Macmillan Publishing Company
866 Third Avenue
New York, NY 10022

Macmillan Publishing Company is part of
the Maxwell Communication Group of Companies.

First published in Great Britain by
Orion Children's Books in 1993

Printed in Italy

10 9 8 7 6 5 4 3 2 1

Library of Congress Catalog Card Number: 93–72433
ISBN 0–689–31920–7

NANNY FOX

Georgie Adams

Illustrated by
Selina Young

Atheneum 1994 New York
Maxwell Macmillan International
New York Oxford Singapore Sydney

Arnold Fox loved chickens.

Not to eat – just as friends.

He spent hours watching the birds scratching about in the farmyard, picking at this, pecking at that, and laying their eggs all over the place.

The Buff Orpingtons were the noisiest hens.
Mrs Buff Orpington fluffed out her feathers to make
herself look bigger and more important than all the rest.
At supper time she would rush about, picking at the
tastiest titbits. Pick, pick, peck!

Arnold loved to see the chicks hatch.

He would hide near a clutch of eggs, listen to the soft
tap, tap, tap inside, then watch as one by one . . . *crack!*
each egg split open and out clambered a tiny yellow
chick, wet and wobbly.

Eating them was unthinkable.

Arnold's family thought differently.

"Chickens are for eating," said Ma Fox, plonking down a fat hen for supper one night.

"It's traditional," said Pa Fox, tucking into a tasty leg.

"And yummy!" said Arnold's sister, Lucy.

"Go on, try some," suggested his brother, Dennis.

"I'll stick to peanut butter sandwiches, thank you," said Arnold.

Pa Fox was puzzled.

"Eating chickens is what foxes do best," he said.

"And catching them is fun!" said Ma Fox.

For weeks Ma Fox had been teaching her children to steal
chickens from the farm. She showed them how to
creep through the woods at night . . .
sneak up to the henhouse . . .
wriggle through a hole . . .
and snatch a sleepy hen or two.

Then, they would dash for cover with the squawking bundles, before the farmer could get out of bed and chase them away.

Poor Arnold was horrified. Hunting expeditions were not for him. Perhaps, he thought sadly, it's time for me to leave home.

One day, as Arnold was passing the henhouse, he saw a notice. It read:

WANTED
KIND NANNY FOR NEW CHICKS
APPLY WITHIN
signed Buff Orpington (mrs.)

He knocked at the door. Mrs Buff Orpington opened it – and fainted.

"I've come about the job," said Arnold when she had recovered. "I'd love to look after your chicks."

"Foxes don't look after chickens," said Mrs Buff Orpington suspiciously. "They eat them."

Arnold thought of his family.
"Some do," he admitted. "But I don't."

Just then, Mrs Buff Orpington's new chicks appeared. They liked the look of Arnold. He was soft and furry and had gentle eyes. They were too young to know about foxes.

Mrs Buff Orpington considered Arnold with care. She was a busy bird and needed help quickly.

"When can you start?" she asked.

"Today," said Arnold.

"Good," said Mrs Buff Orpington. "You'll do. But remember, I've got six chicks. I've counted them . . . twice. And if one should disappear," she said, looking hard at Arnold, "I'll send for the farmer at once."

Arnold went home to pack his bag and say goodbye.

"Where are you going?" asked Ma Fox.

"To the farm," said Arnold.

"What for?" said Pa Fox. "It's not supper time."

"I've got a job," said Arnold.

"What have you got to do?" asked Lucy and Dennis.

"Look after . . . things," said Arnold vaguely.
He couldn't explain about the chicks. His family
would never understand.

So Arnold left home and became Nanny Fox, and the chicks loved him dearly. Keeping all six chicks together was a problem. They wandered off in all directions at once. Arnold spent the first day counting them, again and again. One, two, three, four, five . . . six.

Next day, Arnold found an old bicycle in the barn.
It had a basket on the front, just big enough to hold six chicks.

So they spent the day riding round the farmyard meeting the geese and the goats, the pigs and the cows.

Arnold taught the chicks all kinds of things.
He taught them how to ride on his back,
run egg and spoon races across the field, and . . .

stuff pillows with feathers for a battle at bedtime.
The chicks liked this game. Mrs Buff Orpington did not.
There were feathers all over the henhouse.

That night, as the hens huddled fast asleep, two young foxes came creeping through the shadows. They padded silently round the henhouse and wriggled through a hole.

It was Lucy and Dennis, hunting on their own for the first time.

Then came the most terrible screeching as Dennis snatched Mrs Buff Orpington from her perch and Lucy pulled her into the yard.

Arnold ran to see what was the matter. He found Mrs Buff Orpington being buffeted about like a bean bag.

"She's mine!" cried Lucy, tugging Mrs Buff Orpington to the right.

"I got her first," shouted Dennis, pulling her to the left.

Mrs Buff Orpington squawked at the top of her voice.

"Stop it!" ordered Arnold, flinging himself at Dennis and grabbing Lucy by the ear. "Put her down!"

By this time, all the other animals had woken up.
The geese were honking, the goats were bleating,
the pigs were snorting, and the cows were mooing.

Suddenly, lights went on in the farmhouse. There was
an angry yell from the farmer and the two foxes leapt
apart. Arnold slipped under the henhouse.

Dennis and Lucy ran home and told Ma Fox and Pa Fox what had happened.

"Arnold was guarding the henhouse," said Dennis.

"He pulled my ear," complained Lucy.

Dennis and Lucy didn't mention their quarrel.

"Hm," said Ma Fox thoughtfully. "Now Arnold is at the farm, we shall have to hunt somewhere else."

There was no fat hen for supper that night.

Back at the farm, Mrs Buff Orpington lay in a crumpled heap.
Arnold crawled out from his hiding place and lifted her gently
onto a pile of straw. He smoothed her ruffled feathers.

The frightened chicks clambered out of
the henhouse and gathered round.
Mrs Buff Orpington opened a beady eye
and saw Arnold bending over her.

"Did you just try to eat me?" she croaked.

Arnold shook his head.

"Nanny Fox tried to save you!"
chirped the chicks as they
clung to Arnold's fur.
It was wet and dirty
from the tussle.

Mrs Buff Orpington sighed with relief and Arnold smiled at his brood.

"Nanny Fox loves chickens," he said.
"Not to eat – just as friends!"